T0308489

# Bird Watchers

## CONTENTS

NATIONAL GEOGRAPHIC    Hampton-Brown

School Publishing

# Words with **ow, ou**

Look at each picture. Read the words.

**Example:**

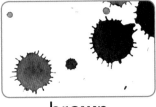

br**ow**n

p**ou**ch

cl**ou**d

**ow**l

playgr**ou**nd

fl**ow**er

# Key Words

Look at the pictures. Read the sentences.

**High Frequency Words**

| |
|---|
| black |
| brown |
| group |
| high |
| leave |
| open |
| point |
| soon |
| study |
| will |

**Owls**

1. Scientists **study** owls, a **group** of birds that hunt for food as they fly.
2. Owls' feathers—with **points** of gray, **brown**, and **black**—help them blend in.
3. Most owls nest **high** up in trees, hidden in the branches.
4. Owls will wait for the sun to go down before they **will leave** their nests.
5. **Soon** they will hunt for food over **open** land.

How do owls' gray, brown, and black points help them blend in?

**Phonics Games**

NGReach.com

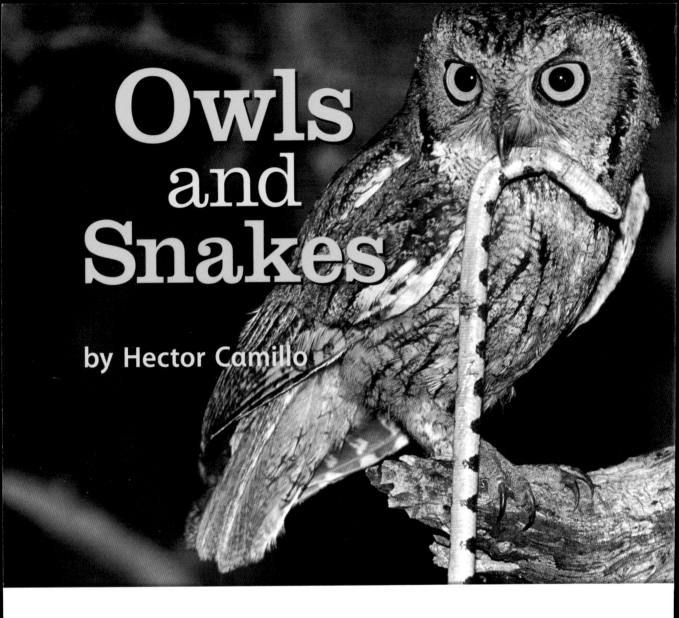

# Owls and Snakes

by Hector Camillo

In most cases, owls and snakes are deadly enemies. Owls will often pounce on and eat snakes. And snakes will often eat owl eggs or owl babies.

However, scientists have found a pair that stand out from this group of enemies. These owls and snakes help each other out. You'll see how this works.

But first, let's meet the snakes in this partnership.

earthworm

Blind snakes look like long earthworms. They are dark brown or grayish black. They are called blind snakes but are not totally blind. Like any snake, their eyes are always open. But these snakes can just see light.

Blind snakes are found under piles of leaves, in flowerpots, and underground. They feed on ants' eggs and termites, and on other insects.

Screech owls are found high up in trees. Their houses are nesting holes made by other kinds of birds. These owls are small. They blend in with their surroundings.

prey

Screech owls have outstanding hearing and even better eyesight. They can hear small animals crouching underneath leaves. A screech owl will fly down from its high perch and pounce on its prey.

However, screech owls will not eat blind
snakes. Instead, they take the snakes back to
their nests and let them go. The blind snakes
may try to get out at first, but soon settle down.
In the screech owl's nest, there is plenty to eat!

Owl nests get quite dirty. Crowds of insects feed on what the screech owls leave behind. These insects, such as flies and ants, can be harmful to baby owls. Blind snakes prowl around and eat these harmful bugs. They clean the nest.

baby owls

Scientists study how animals help each other out. They have found that baby owls have a better chance to survive if blind snakes share their nests.

Scientists point to the screech owl and blind snake as two animals that can count on each other for help.

These owls and snakes might have been powerful enemies. How did they come to help each other instead? We haven't found out yet. Scientists will just have to keep studying them! ❖

# Words with <u>ow</u>, <u>ou</u>

Read these words.

| | | | |
|---|---|---|---|
| groundhog | wolf | prowling | wildcat |
| pouncing | owl | underground | howling |

Find the words with **ow** or **ou**.
Use letters to build them.

o  w  l

**Talk Together**

Choose words from the
box above to tell your partner
about these animals.

The <u>owl</u> is
<u>pouncing</u>.

groundhog

wildcat

# Words with Schwa

Look at each picture. Read the words.

**Example:**

**a**sleep

**a**dult

alarm

**a**wake

**a**fraid

**a**cross

High Frequency
**Words**

black

brown

group

high

leave

open

point

soon

study

will

# Key Words

Look at the pictures. Read the sentences.

**High-Flying Birds**

1. This **group** of birds flies **high** over **open** water.
2. They have **brown** or **black** markings on their wings.
3. The flock may stay on rocky land at a **point** that the birds can **leave** easily.
4. Scientists **study** these birds and **will** **soon** find ways to protect then.

What would it be like to see things from so high up?

**Phonics Games**
NGReach.com

17

# Pelican
# Watch

**by Madeline Rojas**

Sitting on a log on a beach is a perfect spot to study birds. Along the Oregon coast, you can see an amazing number of birds.

gull

black oystercatcher

Sandpipers race across the sand where the waves wash up on the shore. Gulls glide across the sky. Black oystercatchers hunt around the rocks.

Each season brings new groups to the
Oregon coast. Some stop as they migrate.
Others never leave. They will stay around all
year, as long as they can find safe nesting
places—and the amount of food they need.

    One bird that is fun to watch is the pelican. The pelican is a big bird. It is known for the huge pouch under its bill. It uses the pouch to hold the fish that it catches before gulping them down. An adult pelican will eat about four pounds of fish a day.

Pelicans can be seen skimming along in a line at the point where the waves begin to crash. They fly around above the sea, looking for fish. They watch for the light reflecting off the scales of swimming schools, or groups, of fish.

When a brown pelican spots a fish from high up, it will dive for the water. It shoots ahead really fast! Just before it hits the water, it will fold its wings and enter the water like an arrow.

prey

When the brown pelican plunges into the water, it opens its huge bill to catch its prey. It goes down deep to grab a fish. This makes the brown pelican different from other pelicans.

Other pelicans catch fish that swim near the top. Brown pelicans catch fish that swim deeper. This means that brown pelicans don't snatch away fish that other pelicans are hunting.

Some pelicans fish in a group. They form a line out in the water. Then they all flap and splash their wings, chasing the alarmed fish into shallow water. They herd the fish! Each pelican uses its pouch to scoop up a large amount of fish, just like a fisher uses a net.

Gulls know how to use pelicans' amazing fishing skills. A pelican lets the water drain out of its bill after a dive. A gull will sneak up and try to steal away the fish right out of the pouch! A gull may even perch on a pelican's head, grabbing at fish as soon as it gets the chance.

The Oregon coast is alive with birds. They are amazing animals to watch. And a diving brown pelican is an astonishing sight to see! ❖

# Words with Schwa

Read these words.

| across | away | honking | ahead |
|--------|------|---------|-------|
| hunting | around | alarmed | amaze |

Find the words that begin with the sound of **a** in *about*. Use letters to build them.

| a | c | r | o | s | s |
|---|---|---|---|---|---|

**Talk Together**

Choose words from the box above to tell your partner about these different birds.

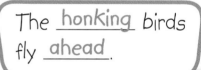

The _honking_ birds fly _ahead_.

# Fly Away Home

Play in a group with two other classmates. Respond to number one below. If your classmates agree that you are right, move your marker one space. If they think you are wrong, do not move. Now it is Player 2's turn to give a different response to number 1. Then Player 3's. Go on to number two. Keep playing until one of you gets home.

1. Name something found along the beach.
2. Name an animal that can growl.
3. Name an animal that lives high up, above the ground.
4. Name something green that can be found outside.
5. Name something little children are often afraid of.
6. Name something that is amazing.
7. Name something that you can open.
8. Point to and name something that is across the room.
9. Name a flower.
10. Name something you will study at school.

Start

Home

**Acknowledgments**
Grateful acknowledgment is given to the authors, artists, photographers, museums, publishers, and agents for permission to reprint copyrighted material. Every effort has been made to secure the appropriate permission. If any omissions have been made or if corrections are required, please contact the Publisher.

**Photographic Credits**
**CVR** (bl) Pavel Semenov/Shutterstock. (tl) Joe McDonald/Visuals Unlimited/Getty Images. (tr) Brian Florky/Shutterstock. **2** (bl) Rick Rhay/iStockphoto. (br) Stockbyte/Getty Images. (cl) Creatas/Jupiterimages. (cr) Corel. (tl) robybret/Shutterstock. (tr) Theo Allofs/Flirt/Corbis. **3** Liz Garza Williams/Hampton-Brown/National Geographic School Publishing. **4** Tom Vezo/Minden Pictures/National Geographic Image Collection. **5** Michael and Patricia Fogden/Minden Pictures/National Geographic Image Collection. **6** PhotoDisc/Getty Images. **7** Joseph T. Collins/Photo Researchers, Inc. **8** Gary Meszaros/Photo Researchers, Inc. **9** Scott Linstead/Minden Pictures. **11** Bill Beatty/Visuals Unlimited. **12** Leonard Lee Rue III/Photo Researchers, Inc. **13** (inset) Robert Valentic/Nature Picture Library. (t) PureStock/SuperStock. **14** Jeff Greenberg/Alamy Images. **15** Liz Garza Williams/Hampton-Brown/National Geographic School Publishing. **16** (b) John Foxx Images/Imagestate. (cl) Dave & Les Jacobs/Getty Images. (cr) Cultura/Alamy Images. (tl) Digital Vision/Getty Images. (tr) Monkey Business Images/Shutterstock. **17** (b) Liz Garza Williams/Hampton-Brown/National Geographic School Publishing. (tl) Tsuneo Nakamura/Volvox Inc/Alamy Images. (tr) Pete Oxford/Minden Pictures. **18-19** (t) Laurence Wolf TIPS RF/Photolibrary. **19** (cr) George Ostertag/SuperStock. (tr) Steve Byland/Shutterstock. **20** Bruce Heinemann/Photodisc/Getty Images. **21** Tim Laman/National Geographic Image Collection. **22** Rich Reid/National Geographic Image Collection. **23** Bill Curtsinger/National Geographic Image Collection. **24** (t) Tui De Roy/Minden Pictures/National Geographic Image Collection. **24-25** (t) Steve Kaufman/Corbis. **26** Mike VanDeWalker/Alamy Images. **27** (t) Robert E. Barber/Alamy Images. **28** Nils Kahle International Photographer/Photographer's Choice/Getty Images. **29** Liz Garza Williams/Hampton-Brown/National Geographic School Publishing.

**Illustrator Credits**
**10** Emily Damstra; **3**, **15**, **29**, **30-31** Peter Grosshauser; **18** Mapping Specialists Ltd.

**The National Geographic Society**
John M. Fahey, Jr., President & Chief Executive Officer
Gilbert M. Grosvenor, Chairman of the Board

National Geographic School Publishing
Hampton-Brown
www.NGSP.com

Printed in the USA.
Quad Graphics, Leominster, MA

ISBN: 978-0-7362-8083-9

18 19 20
10 9 8 7